W9-CCX-276

Everything Is Different at Nonna's House

BY CARON LEE COHEN ILLUSTRATED BY HIROE NAKATA

CLARION BOOKS * NEW YORK

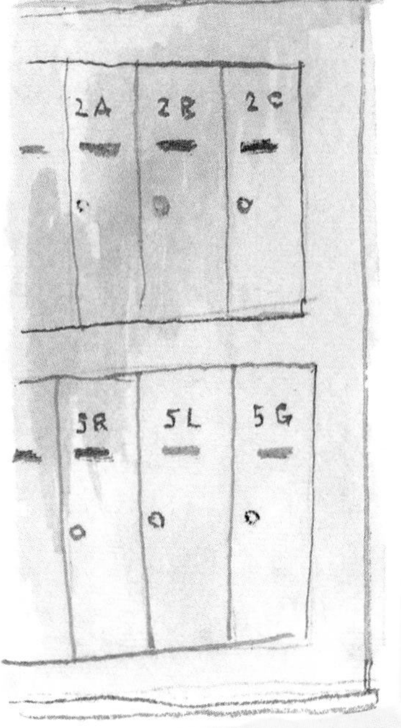

Clarion Books
a Houghton Mifflin Company imprint
215 Park Avenue South, New York, NY 10003

The illustrations were executed in watercolor.
The text was set in 18-point Coop Light.

www.houghtonmifflinbooks.com

Printed in Singapore

Library of Congress Cataloging-in-Publication Data
Cohen, Caron Lee.
Everything is different at Nonna's house / by Caron Lee Cohen; illustrated by Hiroe Nakata.
p. cm.
Summary: A young boy describes the differences between his home in the city and life on his grandparents' farm and learns that no matter where he is their love for him is always the same.
ISBN 0-618-07335-3 (alk. paper)
[1. Grandmothers–Fiction. 2. Country life–Fiction. 3. City and town life–Fiction.] I. Nakata, Hiroe, ill. II. Title.
PZ7.C65974Ev 2003
[E]–dc21
2002009278
TWP 10 9 8 7 6 5 4 3 2 1

Everything is different at Nonna's house.
No honk, honk taxis jam the street.
And no way-up buildings crowd the sky.
At Nonna's house, the yard is wide and quiet.
And the whole blue sky reaches
all the way down to the flower beds.

MYRON'S

For Mina and Pop-Pop,
whose gifts will go on and on

—C.L.C.

For my grandmother

—H.N.

At Nonna's house, there's no rush, rush—go to school, go to work, see you later. When the sun pokes in, it's get-up time, but very slow. Momma smiles, right there, and never goes away.

Then hug, hug, hug—Pop-Pop twirls me in the air. And kiss, kiss, kiss—Nonna says, "*Mmmmmmmmmmm, my big boy!*" And happy, laughy words spill all around.

At Nonna's house, we don't grab the toast and run. There's always time for blueberry pancakes. I stand on a chair and stir the batter all by myself. And the blueberries come with a kiss. I make the best pancakes! Nonna says so.

At Nonna's house, we don't get flowers at the corner shop. They grow right outside the kitchen door. I water them with the big watering can. I have to use two hands to hold it. I'm so strong at Nonna's house!

At Nonna's house, I don't ride the elevator with Mr. Grotz. Instead, I ride the tractor with Pop-Pop. Sometimes I turn the great big steering wheel all by myself. I'm a big helper. Pop-Pop says so.

I climb the stepladder with Nonna and clip the roses. I can do it! I wave to Momma from way up high, and she looks all smiley and waves back. I'm such a big boy at Nonna's house!

At Nonna's house, there's no Myron's Deli down the street. But there are moo cows. They stand in the grass and switch their tails. I tell Nonna they eat french fries. She says, no, they eat their vegetables raw. And we laugh and laugh.

At Nonna's house, I don't have to go to bed when it's dark. We stay out late at night on the porch. We watch the stars blink. We hear the crickets in the yard and the peepers in the woods. We sit together, close and cozy. We are warm like that even when the night is cool.

Tonight Nonna and I go for a walk. And there—bigger than

I ever saw it before, all silvery, all light—the moon! "Look, Nonna!"

I put my hands up, and the whole moon fits into them.
"I can hold it! Right here! See? The whole sky is different.
Everything is different at your house."

"We have a wonderful sky,"
Nonna says. "But it's the same sky all over. And it's
the same moon everywhere, even when you can't see it."

"No, it's different here," I tell her. "At your house, I'm a big boy!"

“It doesn’t matter where you are,” Nonna says. “You’re the same big boy. And no matter where we are, we love you, even when we’re far away. Remember that.”

On the train back home, I remember.

And at the corner shop, the flowers are smiling like the ones at Nonna's kitchen door, and I remember.

MYRON'S

And at my way-up building, Mr. Grotz says, "Glad you're back!" And happy, sunny words fill the elevator.

So I just tell him, "You know what? It's the same sky everywhere. And I'm the same big boy."

And in my cozy room, through my window, there's the moon.
"Look, Momma, I can hold it, just like at Nonna's house."
"Yes," she says. "What a big boy you are!"